Chessie walked slowly down the hall, her cookie boxes clutched in her arms, her Girl Scout hat perched neatly on top of her dark, glossy hair. She was scared to death. She would never have admitted it to the boys, not for a second, but she was really frightened. She had insisted on being the one to go; she had come up with the idea of dressing in her Girl Scout uniform. She had even convinced herself that the acting she had done for her father and Sergeant Gauss had whetted her appetite for this job. But now, as she walked down the hallway, she was not so sure. What if she couldn't even get near the computer room? Bobbie had shown her where it was, even drawn her a map, but what if she never made it past the receptionist? What if she fumbled and they caught her trying to place the black box under the terminal? What would they do to her then?

MILTON DANK is the author of several novels for young adult readers, including *The Dangerous Game*, *Game's End*, (available in Dell Laurel-Leaf editions) *Khaki Wings*, and *Red Flight Two*. *The Computer Caper* and its companion novel, *A UFO Has Landed*, written in collaboration with his daughter Gloria, are the first two books in the Galaxy Gang Mystery series.

GLORIA DANK was graduated from Princeton University with a bachelor's degree in psychology and has worked as a computer analyst. She is currently writing a fantasy novel.

Milton Dank and Gloria Dank live and work in suburban Philadelphia.

A Galaxy Gang Mystery

The Computer Caper

Milton Dank & Gloria Dank

LAUREL-LEAF BOOKS

LAUREL-LEAF BOOKS bring together under a single imprint outstanding works of fiction and nonfiction particularly suitable for young adult readers, both in and out of the classroom. Charles F. Reasoner, Professor Emeritus of Children's Literature and Reading, New York University, is consultant to this series.

Published by
Dell Publishing Co., Inc.
1 Dag Hammarskjold Plaza
New York, New York 10017

This work is simultaneously published in a hardcover edition by Delacorte Press, New York, New York.

Laurel-Leaf Library ® TM 766734,
Dell Publishing Co., Inc.

ISBN: 0-440-91139-7

RL: 5.7

Printed in the United States of America

First Laurel-Leaf printing—December 1983

be trouble tomorrow."

Bobbie fanned herself limply. "It's too hot to make trouble."

The gang agreed. It was a heavy, late-summer day. Even in the shade of the trees the heat made their clothes cling. In the distance a brownish haze shrouded the Philadelphia skyline. The air was still y down the street.

"What do you think that was all about?" Diggy.

"Gangs," Sphinx said. "Now that started, the police are watching out gangs. You know, like the Centurions, and the Red Barons."

1

☐ "Look! Those policemen are watching us!"

Alerted by Bobbie's urgent whisper, her three companions stopped eating and turned to stare. Near the entrance to the little city park a squad car had stopped, and the two officers inside were looking up at the four teenagers on the grassy slope. Chessie smiled and waved at them. Sphinx returned to his pizza, and Diggy tried to appear unconcerned. After a few minutes the squad c̶ moved slowly dow̶

"But," Diggy protested, "the Galaxy Gang's not like that. We're different."

Chessie shook her head. "There are so many gangs in the schools. And most of them are always in trouble. Shoplifting and worse . . . ripping off gold chains from women walking through the neighborhood. Lots of crazy stuff."

"How come you know so much about what's going on?" Diggy asked.

The pretty, dark-haired girl drained the last of her soft drink before answering. "My father knows a lot of policemen, and my cousin, Angela, is dating officer Cassidy. You know, the one who guards the crossing at Pell Street. The good-looking one." Diggy and Sphinx made cooing sounds, but Francesca Morelli just smiled her madonna smile and went on. "Anyway, the police are under a lot of pressure to do something about teenage gangs."

"But why us?" Diggy complained. "We've never done anything like that."

"All kids look alike to the cops," said Chessie. "They figure that if we're not trouble today, we'll and burning, and the boys and girls longed for a breeze.

They stretched out on the grass, enjoying the companionship they had missed during summer vacation. The heat made them drowsy, and soon the talk dwindled. Every once in a while someone would sit up and look toward the park entrance. The fifth member of their gang, Larry Strauss, was late.

Chessie giggled, and the others looked at her. "Can you imagine the report those two policemen will turn in? All about spotting the Galaxy Gang in their hideout plotting all sorts of terrible crimes."

Laughing, Diggy began the "report": "At four twelve P.M. on Tuesday, September fifth, Officers A and B were on patrol in the vicinity of Washington Square Park. Four members of the notorious Galaxy Gang were spotted by the alert officers. The gang was observed to be eating what appeared to be pizza. Positively identified was Oliver Osgood the Third, known as 'Sphinx,' wanted in three states for running the numbers racket and turning in his homework on time. With his hair dyed red to complete his disguise as a top math student, this well-known criminal is a fugitive from the local Science Fair and the FBI Math Competition."

"Look, boss," Sphinx whined, "how did I know the cops would finger me?"

"Geez," Bobbie snarled, "don't you know nuttin'?

It's easy for a beanpole like you to duck the fuzz. Just turn sideways, and they'll never see you!"

Chessie continued the report. "Sphinx was seen getting his orders from a sandy-haired, round-faced character, the mastermind of the mob, Digby 'Diggy' Caldwell. Believed to be the brains behind the Brinks armored car heist and the Bank of Paris safe job, Caldwell is suspected of lifting two custard pies from a bakery truck last week. No pie tins were observed in the gang's present hideout in the park."

"Also at the scene," said Sphinx, "was 'Chessie' Morelli, the gang moll, known to hang around good-looking police officers to get information for the mob. Morelli's buddy, Bobbie Leinsdorf, known as the 'Fearless Fräulein,' was also present. As the police approached, the gang slipped into the shade of the old apple tree."

Diggy looked up at the overhanging branches. "Poplar?"

"Well, they're not popular with the police," said Sphinx with a grin. There was a loud volley of boos.

"I don't know which is harder to take," Chessie complained, "your puns or Larry's quotations. You should both be arrested and jailed."

"And speaking of Larry," Bobbie said, "here he comes now—and he's not alone."

They all stood up, brushing themselves off, as

Larry and another boy ran up the slope. "Something's up," Diggy muttered. Bringing a stranger to a meeting of the gang was almost unheard of.

As the two newcomers arrived under the trees, Larry threw out his arms and shouted, " 'I travel for travel's sake. The great affair is to move.' Robert Louis Stevenson." He collapsed on the ground, then waved a hand at the other boy. "Gang, this is Tilo."

The tall, slender Oriental boy lowered his head shyly. Diggy invited him to sit down.

"Tilo came to me because I'm his only American friend," Larry explained from his prone position. "His family is in big trouble."

"What trouble?" Chessie asked.

Tilo looked at Larry, cleared his throat, and then began to speak in a low, soft voice with a slight accent. At times they had to lean forward to catch his words.

"My name is Ti Long Xuan"—he pronounced it "Kwang"—"and I live on South Street. My family owns the tailor shop next to the hardware store. Two years ago we came from Vietnam, from a small village named Lan Duc. Everything was strange to us, so different from what we knew over there. It was hard at first, but we do not complain."

Tilo paused and groped for words. "My father and mother worked very hard so that my sister, my brother, and I would have a better life. My father

5

is a good tailor, and my mother sews also. The shop did well, and we saved our money. Not a fortune, you understand, everything costs so much, but for us it was a lot. My father dreamed of buying a bigger shop, even hiring an assistant to help him with the work."

There was another pause.

"Then a man came to our house, a big man with silver hair, very impressive. He talked well. He told my father that the savings could be invested in a wonderful company, something to do with finding oil. I don't think my father really understood what it was all about, but the man promised we would make a lot of money. My father was blinded by this man's words. He signed some papers and gave this man, Oscar Baring, all our savings. I think he felt that it must be safe, since the law would never allow anyone to do anything illegal—not so openly."

Why is it we all know how this is going to turn out? Diggy asked himself. He hated to ask the obvious question.

"When did your father learn the truth?"

"About two months later. My father went to Baring's office, and a man named Phillips told him that the company he had invested in was bankrupt, and all the money was lost. My father was in tears and tried to see the man Baring, but Phillips kept say-

details: what Baring promised, how the money was handed over, and especially the name of the company that's supposed to have gone bust. Oh yes, and get the name of that lawyer who was so 'helpful.' Maybe he's part of the whole swindle."

"Actually," Sphinx said, "we don't know that it is a swindle. People do lose money in bad investments, you know. My father did—a pot of money."

The famous Spock logic was Sphinx's strong point. In their haste to help Tilo, the gang had immediately assumed the worst. But what if Baring was innocent?

Diggy settled the matter. "If Mr. Xuan wasn't cheated, then there's nothing wrong in finding that out. And if he was, we'll still have to prove it. No one else is helping Tilo's family right now."

After talking over a few more details, they arranged to meet during lunch the next day. As they walked out of the park Larry was talking quietly to Tilo, reassuring him. The Galaxy Gang was going into action. As Diggy's father, a lieutenant commander in the U.S. Navy, would have said, it was time for battle stations.

□

The desk sergeant at the Tenth Precinct station looked suspiciously at the pretty, dark girl and the husky, towheaded boy who had just asked for Sergeant Gauss. Teenagers, his stern gaze seemed to say, were trouble.

"He's busy," the desk sergeant said. "Better call him or write a letter. What's the matter, kids? Did someone steal your lunch money?"

Chessie smiled like an angel while Diggy scowled.

"No, sir, it's more important than that," she said. "Sergeant Gauss is a good friend of my father's, and I'm sure he'll want to talk to us. And you'd like to help us too, wouldn't you?" She smiled again while Diggy looked a little disgusted.

The desk sergeant shuffled his papers.

"Second floor, turn right," he said at last. "In the squad room."

The squad room was large and filled with desks, ringing telephones, and the odor of stale tobacco smoke. A detective interrupted his questioning of a suspect to listen to their question, then pointed to the back. The two teenagers wended their way between the desks, followed by the stares of the police officers. Diggy felt ill at ease, but Chessie seemed perfectly comfortable. She had been here before with her father.

A heavyset man with graying hair, thick eyebrows, and large hands was hunched over a typewriter. Diggy noticed that his nose was broken and wondered how it had happened.

As the two teenagers approached, Gauss looked up and grinned.

"*Francesca! Come sta?*" he bellowed with delight. Sergeant Gauss had spent twenty years as a cop in this mixed neighborhood, and he spoke a half-dozen different languages.

"*Bene, molto bene, Sergente,*" Chessie replied. "This is my friend, Diggy Caldwell."

Diggy held out his hand. "Happy to meet you, Sergeant."

The detective grunted and shook hands briefly. "What are you doing here, Francesca? You're not in any trouble, are you?"

Chessie shook her head.

"It's not me, Sergeant. It's a friend of ours. His family's been cheated out of their savings by a fast-talking con man." She told him the story of the Xuan family and Oscar Baring just as Tilo had told it.

Gauss leaned back in his chair and listened without interrupting. Twice he shook his head. It was clear that he had heard similar stories many times before. When Chessie explained why Mr. Xuan was afraid to go to the police, the sergeant growled: "This isn't Vietnam, and we're not the Viet police. I'd like to help, Francesca, but without some proof we can't do a thing. Frankly I don't think your friends have much of a chance of getting their money back. I'm assuming, of course, that this was really a swindle, and not just a case of poor business judgment. Even if Mr. Xuan filed a complaint, proof that Baring cheated him would be practically impossible to get. What these guys do is set up a dummy company, transfer all the money out of it, then claim it went bankrupt. But how do we prove that it was a dummy company? Baring would be too smart to leave written records around for us to find. No, the only proof would be hidden away somewhere where only Baring could get his hands on it."

Chessie's face fell.

"Can't the police at least look into it?" Diggy asked. "It's wrong to let these people get swindled without anyone even lifting a finger to help them!"

"Without a complaint we can't do anything." Gauss pointed to a stack of folders on his desk. "You see those? Well, each one is an investigation that I'm responsible for. Each one means hours on the streets looking for evidence, and they're all serious crimes—burglaries, holdups, assaults, rapes. If Mr. Xuan came in today and swore out a complaint against Baring, you know what'd happen to it? It'd go to the bottom of that pile and wait its turn. And every other detective in this room has that many cases or more. We're just overloaded. Too many crimes and not enough policemen. Sorry."

Diggy's face was slowly turning scarlet. "I suppose Mr. Xuan would have to get himself killed to get any attention from the police!"

"That's not fair, kiddo. You know that. Your

"Not at all," said Sphinx grandly, following him in.

They walked down a short hallway toward the receptionist. The man smiled as the two teenagers crowded behind him.

"Does your father work here?" he asked Sphinx. Sphinx motioned toward the receptionist.

"My aunt," he said.

"Aah," nodded the man.

They entered the room, and the man walked up to the reception desk. Sphinx and Bobbie glanced around and then seated themselves side by side on a couch next to the wall.

The receptionist glanced up at the man and the two kids. She smiled. Sphinx and Bobbie smiled back. The man looked at her and at the two teenagers, and smiled. The woman smiled at him.

"May I help you?" she asked.

"Yes, I'd like some more information about these sheltered Mexican bank accounts." The man produced a glossy brochure from a folder.

"I see. One minute, please." She picked up the phone and spoke into it in low tones. When she finished, she said, "It's the first door on your left. Mr. Josephson will be happy to answer any questions you might have."

"Thank you very much." The man gathered up his papers and, with a friendly glance at the kids, disappeared around the corner. The receptionist turned back to them.

"We'll just wait here," Sphinx offered.

"Fine," she replied. "Make yourselves comfortable. Is that your father?"

"Our uncle," Sphinx said.

"I see," said the woman, returning to her typing.

Sphinx and Bobbie stared around them. It was a large room containing the secretary's desk, two couches with side-tables, four file cabinets, and several bookshelves. The only exits were the way they had come and the corridor that branched off to their right. Sphinx picked up a company brochure from one of the side-tables and began to leaf through it.

Bobbie cleared her throat. "May I use the ladies' room?" she asked.

"Of course," replied the receptionist. "It's down that hallway, last door on your right."

"Thank you." Bobbie rose, and walked in the direction their "uncle" had gone.

Sphinx sighed and settled back into his seat. They had decided beforehand that any exploring should be done by Bobbie—one person was less likely to attract interest than two people snooping around the office. No one would suspect a young girl with blond braids of being up to no good.

Sphinx folded the brochure and stuck it in his pocket.

"Nice office you have here," he said to the receptionist.

"Thank you."

"Do a lot of people work here?"

"No, not really," she said. "It's just myself, Mr. Phillips, Mr. Josephson, and, of course, Mr. Baring." She twinkled at him. "Why? Are you interested in applying for a position?"

"Why, yes," said Sphinx with dignity. "In about ten years."

The receptionist laughed.

"We'll look forward to it," she said.

□

Bobbie walked down the hallway, looking carefully around her. She paused by the first door on the left—Mr. Josephson's room—and heard the sound of voices. Their adopted uncle must be in there. Bobbie wished him luck—from what she knew of Baring's investments, he might need it. The door of the office directly across the hall had a sign— SAMUEL T. PHILLIPS. She continued down the corridor. In the next room to the left there was a rapid clickety-click of some kind of machine . . . a typewriter? No, it was too fast . . . a Teletype or a computer, maybe? Behind the door on the other side there was silence. The same with the next office on the left. The last office to the right had a name neatly painted on the wall next to it, in gold letters: OSCAR BARING. Bobbie paused and listened, but either it was empty or Baring was keeping very quiet. The next door was the ladies' room.

Once inside, she reviewed the office setup. Then she washed her hands and quickly checked her reflection in the mirror.

It's no problem for me to look younger than I am, she thought, surveying her braids. Chessie, maybe, but not me. Oh, well. Now, let's see . . . on the left side of the hall is Josephson's room, then a room with a computer or Teletype in it, and then . . .

A few minutes later she emerged into the corridor and started back.

"I don't know how in the world Diggy expects us to find a safe, if there is one," she thought. "What are we supposed to do, sneak into every room in the place?"

She was almost back in the outer office when she suddenly halted. The door of Phillips's office opened. A small, thin man walked down the hallway, his back to her, and knocked on Baring's door. He waited a moment and then went in.

Turning, Bobbie stole down the corridor and paused outside Baring's door. She looked around nervously. What if he comes out again in a minute and finds me standing here?

There was a murmur of voices from inside. Bobbie leaned closer, her head against the door.

"I bet I could hear something if my heart would just stop pounding," she thought.

". . . impossible, impossible," said a deep voice from the other side of the door. ". . . out of your mind, Phillips?"

A low murmur answered him. There was a short silence; then the mumbles began again. Holding her breath, Bobbie strained to hear.

". . . see, you've got to . . . it's illegal . . . I'm afraid that . . ." said Phillips's voice.

Silence. Then Baring responded, his voice sharp and angry.

"You *are* out of your mind," he said furiously. "What are you worried about?"

Mumble, mumble, mumble, responded Phillips. Baring's answer was curt. Then Phillips's voice came clearly through the door.

"I'm not happy about it," he said stubbornly. "Suppose they get into the computer?"

". . . impossible . . . no way . . . we are the . . . remember that . . ." said Baring.

There was another silence.

"All right," Phillips said. "But if there's . . . you know that . . . I'm not going to jail for . . ."

"Stop worrying!"

There was a murmur and a squeak of chairs. Baring opened the door.

He almost ran into a girl with yellow braids coming down the hall. The door to the ladies' room was just swinging shut.

The girl stared at him. "Excuse *me*," snapped Bobbie, brushing past the two men.

"Hey!" cried Baring. "Wait a minute!"

Bobbie stopped and turned around.

"Little girl," said Baring, "what are you doing here?"

Bobbie smiled sweetly.

"I'm waiting for my uncle," she explained. "He's doing some business here."

"Isn't Uncle Herbie done yet?" asked another young voice. A tall, red-headed boy came around the corner, and glanced from Baring to the girl.

"Excuse me," Sphinx said. Taking Bobbie's hand, he led her back into the lobby.

Baring followed them to the front desk.

"Selma," he asked, "Do you know these kids?"

The woman looked up in surprise.

"Why, yes, Mr. Baring," she said. "Their uncle is in talking to Mr. Josephson about an investment."

"Oh," said Baring. Turning, he smiled at Bobbie and Sphinx.

"That's okay, then," he said. "Sorry. You see, I don't usually find kids in my office."

"That's all right," said Bobbie. She stared at Baring's back as he left the lobby.

Sphinx squeezed her hand. "You okay?" he mumbled.

She nodded.

They sat there for what seemed like an eternity. Finally Josephson's door opened and they heard their "uncle" say "Thank you."

"Not at all. Hope to hear from you soon," said the clerk.

Bobbie and Sphinx rose to their feet as the balding man came back to the receptionist's desk. Once again everyone smiled at each other. The man put on his hat and coat and said "Good-bye!" as he walked toward the front door.

"Good-bye," said Selma, and smiled at the "good-byes" from the teenagers as they followed the man down the hall.

"Good-bye, kids," she said.

The man looked surprised as Sphinx held the door open for him again.

"This is some service," he said, shaking his head. "Tell me, does your aunt pay you to do this?" Stepping out onto the sidewalk, he waved and went off down the street.

Bobbie and Sphinx watched him go. Then they moved off in the opposite direction.

When they reached the corner, Sphinx could stand it no longer. Turning, he raised his hand and waved it madly.

"So long, Uncle Herbie!" he shouted, before Bobbie dragged him out of sight.

3

☐ The second day of school separated the Galaxy Gang. They sat through morning classes impatiently. Now, shortly after noon, they were sitting with Tilo in the back of the noisy lunchroom, eating tuna fish sandwiches and listening to Bobbie.

". . . and we got out of the office okay," Bobbie ended her report, "except that Sphinx almost ruined it by yelling good-bye to Uncle Herbie." She glared at the lanky redhead.

"What about the safe?" Diggy asked.

Sphinx shook his head. "No safe. This guy is very modern. I picked up one of his brochures. It says he keeps all his records in a computer."

Bobbie nodded. "I could hear the sounds of a terminal behind one of the doors when I first went down the hall," she explained, "and from what I

24

heard of their conversation, Phillips was very nervous about someone getting '*into the computer*.'"

"What's a terminal?" asked Chessie.

"It's just a keyboard that connects to a main computer somewhere else through the telephone lines," said Sphinx. "Baring doesn't have his own computer—too expensive. He's buying time on one. All his records are in the memory of a computer downtown. Whenever he wants to put something in or get it out, he types the instructions on his terminal."

Diggy looked up. "There's a terminal in the computer room here at school. Can we use it to get the proof we need?"

Sphinx shrugged. "Baring uses the same computer the school does—it says so in the brochure. That's a stroke of luck for us. But even so, we can't get to his records without knowing his account number and password—and I don't think Baring's going to just hand them to us. That stuff is as safe as if it were in Fort Knox."

There was a long silence.

"Is that it?" Larry asked. "Can you do anything?"

Sphinx leaned back and took a huge gulp of soda. "Maybe yes, maybe no."

"C'mon," said Diggy, "what does that mean?"

"It means I have some work to do in the computer room before I know for sure whether it's hopeless or not."

"And how long do you think that will take?"

Sphinx stared at the ceiling. "If I'm lucky, two or three hours. If I'm not lucky, forever." He gazed out the window.

Diggy sighed. He knew when his friend would not be pushed. "Okay, Sphinx, do your best."

"What about the police?" Bobbie asked. "Can't they get into the computer?"

"No," said Diggy, "not without convincing a judge that a crime's been committed. And we can't prove that without Baring's records." He stood up and put his plate and glass on the tray. "We just can't depend on the police. Sergeant Gauss will try his best, because Chessie sweet-talked him with her famous lasagna, but Baring is too smart. Sphinx, it's up to you. We meet in the clubhouse at eight tonight. Tilo, too, of course. See you later."

□

The bell for the last class had just finished ringing when Sphinx strolled into the computer room. Mr. Henderson, the math teacher, peered over his glasses and smiled. "Putting in some overtime, Oliver?" He allowed certain students to work on their programs after school.

"Yes, sir. I had an idea for my project I'd like to check."

"Go right ahead. Just close the door behind you and remember to turn off the master switch." He gathered up his papers, stuffed them into his brief-case, and left.

Sphinx sat down at the terminal and switched it on. Slowly, carefully, he typed out the instructions to call up a program stored in the central com-puter. As the terminal displayed the first lines of his program he leaned forward, his face intent. This was something he had worked out long ago, but had been afraid to use. He had stored it in the computer memory and left it alone. He still didn't know whether it would work, but he was about to find out.

He directed the computer to run the program, and sat back to wait. He was glad that Mr. Hender-son had left. He would have tried to help him with his work, and Sphinx didn't want anyone else to see this. He waited for a few minutes, his eyes on the ceiling, and then sat up as the printer began to chatter.

He went over and tore off the first few pages of printout, scanning them. He went over them, care-fully, twice . . . and then began to smile.

"If I were a crook," he said aloud, "right now I'd be about to become a very rich crook."

He waited until the printer was finished, and then turned off the master switch. Tearing off the printed pages, he put them between the covers of his notebook and left.

As the door closed behind him, he repeated to himself, "A very, very rich crook!"

□

At eight o'clock sharp the gang and Tilo met in the clubhouse, a semidetached garage on Fitzwater Street. It belonged to Judge Thomas Jarrell, a widower who had recently retired from the bench. The tall, white-haired judge was a close friend of Larry's father, who had introduced him to the gang. When Diggy had approached him about using his garage as their clubhouse, the judge had been delighted, saying, "It's like having a whole new family." He had no car, so the garage was empty except for a few pieces of old furniture.

Diggy got straight to the point. "Okay, Sphinx, what's the story? Did it work out?"

Sphinx cleared his throat and looked around at the circle of expectant faces.

"Yep," he said. "It worked. I can get into Baring's records—or anyone else's who uses that computer."

"Fantastic!" Chessie cried.

"How'd you do it?" Larry asked.

"Genius," Sphinx said. "Genius, and the mind of a master criminal."

Bobbie was shaking her head. "You said that only Baring could get into the files."

"C'mon, tell us how you did it," Diggy said.

Sphinx glanced around and smiled. "That's an expensive setup Baring has," he said. "The terminal and computer time aren't cheap. So he's got to use it a lot. And every time he uses it, he has to type the account number and password at the beginning . . . every time, maybe ten or twelve times a day."

"So?" Bobbie said. "What's your idea?"

Sphinx reached into his pocket and took out a small black box about the size of a pack of cigarettes. Handing it to Larry, Sphinx asked, "Can you put a pulser inside of that? One that will run on a battery?"

Puzzled, Larry took the box, opened it, and studied the inside. He tapped the metal case and thought for a moment. "Yeah, I think so. It'll be tight, but there's a new microcircuit I saw in a magazine that should do the job. It's a beaut, and I know where I can get one. What's it for?"

Sphinx gave the smile that had earned him his name. Pointing to the box, he said, "That's all we need to get the info. That, and somebody to stick it under Baring's terminal without getting caught!"

There was a baffled silence. Sphinx beamed at the puzzled looks.

"I ran a program today," he explained. "It's something I worked out months ago but never tried before. It lets me read *all* the other terminals— whatever goes into the central computer. Anything they send in I can read off the school's printer."

"Great," Chessie said. "So from that we can get the password."

"Well, it's not that easy—not yet, anyway."

"But you said. . ."

"Look, there must be hundreds of other terminals using that same computer downtown. I can read all the messages they send out, yeah, but how do we know which one is Baring's?"

"Can't we try them all?" Diggy asked.

Sphinx shrugged. "Sure, but if we're looking for a dummy corporation we'll have to search all the files of everyone who has an account there, and hope there's something identifying Baring's records. That really would take forever."

"So what good is your program?" Bobbie asked.

"The pulser," Sphinx explained, "puts extra spaces in a message and makes it easy to spot on the printout. The account number and password are always at the beginning, so if we get this box onto Baring's terminal, we've got it. Of course, we'll have to be at the school's terminal when Baring sends a message."

"Wait a minute," Larry protested. "Those extra spaces will foul things up. The computer won't recognize the access code, and Baring will know something's wrong."

"Well, he'll probably just think his terminal's gone flaky," Sphinx said. "But by that time we'll have the password. We'll have to get the pulser out of there before a repairman arrives, though."

Diggy pondered the plan. "It's risky," he said. "We'll have to be lucky twice. It will mean making two trips into the office."

Outside the garage the street lights went on, reminding them that it was getting late and that they would have to be home soon. Diggy sat and listened as Sphinx and Larry discussed how the pulser would be attached to the terminal. (They agreed that a magnet glued to the black box was best.) Bobbie and Chessie chatted with Tilo.

"By the way," Sphinx said, "who's going to be the lucky one who puts the box under Baring's terminal?"

"Well, you and Bobbie have already been in Baring's office, so you're out," replied Diggy. "Larry has to build and test the pulser. Tilo might be recognized, so it's either Chessie or me." He hated the idea of sending someone else to do it, but he knew that Chessie was a better actor than he was. He had seen how easily she had softened up Sergeant Gauss.

"I'd like to do it," Chessie said eagerly. "I'm sure I can find an excuse for getting in and out of the office."

Diggy shook his head. "Let me think about it, Chess." He had not forgotten the sergeant's warning. Maybe he should go himself and take his chances on bluffing it through.

"We've got another problem," he went on. "All

this is against the law, gang. You know that as well as I do."

"Actually," said Sphinx, "we don't break any laws until we use the password to get into the files. Isn't that right?"

"Well, I guess so," Diggy said slowly. "But maybe I should go and ask the judge what he thinks before we go ahead."

There was a chorus of "*No*'s."

"Look," said Bobbie, "we don't even know yet whether this is going to work. Sphinx could be wrong, or Larry may not be able to build the pulser, or—or who knows? I don't think we should bother the judge until it's really necessary."

"We may not be able to get the box in and out of the office—no offense, Chess," Sphinx added hastily. "Why don't we wait until we're sure we can get the password?"

Diggy thought it over. "Okay," he said. "Let's see how the plan works. But before we actually break into Baring's files, I'm going to talk to the judge. Is that okay with everybody?"

They nodded.

"Fine." Diggy stood up and stretched. "Meeting's over." They left the garage reluctantly. Diggy turned off the light and closed the garage door. As he followed the others down the quiet street he looked back at the house and saw the light on in the judge's study.

Yes, the judge was their man. He would decide when the time came.

□

As soon as she got to her house, Chessie knew that something was up. Sergeant Gauss's dented Camaro was parked at the curb, and her mother was peering anxiously through the window. Her kid brother was sitting cross-legged on the porch, a mischievous grin on his chubby face. Chessie knew that look all too well. Little Frankie had always resented the way that Chessie could get anything she wanted from their father and would be delighted if she was in trouble. She took a halfhearted swing at the grinning imp, who ducked and rolled out of the way, giggling. Her mother opened the door.

"Francesca, what's going on? Sergeant Gauss is in with your father right now. They want to see you."

Chessie muttered something under her breath and patted her mother's arm. "Oh, I'm sure it's nothing, Mother. I went to see the sergeant to get some information I need for school." Well, she thought, that's not a total lie. "Maybe he has it now and just wanted an excuse to talk to Dad."

Mrs. Morelli stepped aside and let her daughter pass. "Frankie," she said through the open door, "stop making those disgusting noises and come inside!"

In the living room Chessie found her father standing in front of the fireplace, smoking a cigar. The sergeant was seated on the sofa, sipping a glass of wine. He looked up as she entered and went over to kiss her father's cheek. Mr. Morelli shook his head.

"Francesca," he asked, "what's all this that the sergeant has been telling me? How in the world did you get mixed up with this man Baring?"

Chessie bit her lip. She glanced around at the sergeant, who avoided her gaze; then, sitting down on the sofa, she launched into the whole story of Tilo and his family.

"Oh, Dad, it's so unfair! These poor people come to this country for refuge, and what happens? A crook like Baring robs them of every cent they have. And then the police claim that nothing can be done"—Sergeant Gauss choked loudly on his drink—"even though it's just as if Baring had stuck a gun in Mr. Xuan's ribs and taken the money from him by force. We're just trying to help a friend, that's all!"

Her father listened thoughtfully. When Chessie had finished, he cleared his throat and glanced over at Gauss.

"That doesn't sound bad, Marty—trying to help this kid and his family. But why do Francesca and her friends have to get involved? Why can't the police handle it?"

"The guy's got no record . . . at least, not in this state. No evidence of fraud, not even a complaint. Yes, I know, Chessie, Mr. Xuan is scared of policemen, but the fact is that we can't act without a complaint. But at this point I doubt even that would help. This Baring covers his tracks pretty well—if he *is* a thief."

Mr. Morelli puffed at his cigar. "That's it, then, Francesca. If the police can't do anything until there's proof, then you're not to interfere. I understand your concern for your friend, but I don't want you mixed up in this. I don't like the sound of this man Baring, and I do *not* want my daughter to have anything to do with him. Understood?"

Chessie nodded, her eyes downcast. "Until there is proof," her father had said. Well, that was exactly what the Galaxy Gang was after. Of course, she hadn't mentioned Sphinx's plan—that was too much of a long shot right now. Better to wait and see if it would work. Then she'd worry about whether she had the right to disobey her father.

Mr. Morelli beamed. He was not unhappy at what he had heard tonight, but he was even happier at how easily his daughter had accepted his orders.

"Please see the sergeant to the door, Francesca. I have to make some telephone calls. Good night, Marty, and thanks for dropping in."

With a grunt that could have meant anything, Gauss lumbered to his feet, shook hands with Mr.

Morelli, and went to the door with Chessie.

As he stopped in the hallway to collect his cap the sergeant admired a large painting of medieval Florence. Without turning around, he asked casually, "What were your two friends doing in Baring's office yesterday, Chessie? Making some investments, right?"

Chessie felt her heart stop. Her face flushed crimson. "My friends?"

"Why, yes. The skinny redhead—Sphinx, isn't it? —and the tall blond girl. I asked the patrolman on that beat to keep an eye on the office. He happened to notice your friends coming out yesterday afternoon, along with a guy named Herbert."

"Dr. Herbert," said Chessie, "yes, our social science teacher. He's been taking a few of us on field trips to see how industry and finance work in the city. Last week we made a real interesting trip to the Stock Exchange. . ."

"Okay, Francesca, that's a good try, and you're a very clever young lady . . . but remember what I said about Baring not being anyone to fool with. Leave this to the police." Gauss smiled, put on his cap, and went down the steps to his car.

Her heart still pounding, Chessie closed the door and let out a big sigh.

□

It took Larry all his spare time for almost a week to finish the black box. One of the parts was nearly impossible to find in a small enough size, and he had almost given up when another electronics freak told him about a new retail outlet. Sure enough, the owner came up with the part, and also gave Larry some excellent hints on circuit design. Assembling the pulser was an agonizing, almost impossible task. Every solder joint was a triumph of manual skill, concentration, and luck. When it was done, Larry sealed the box to keep water and dirt out, and glued a thin magnetic plate to the top. Then he put it in a large envelope and went to meet Diggy.

Diggy admired the job. "Thanks, Larry," he said, taking the pulser and examining it. Then he stuck it in his pocket. It was time to face the first of his two problems.

Who would do the job, he or Chessie?

4

□ Two days later Chessie stood in front of the door of Baring's office. People on their way back from lunch were thronging all around her on the busy street. No one paid her the slightest attention.

She glanced over to make sure her friends were ready. On the park bench across the street, their faces hidden in the shade of the overhanging trees, Diggy and Sphinx sat watching. As she turned around to face the front door again she could feel their eyes upon her.

Oh, well, she thought. Here goes! Pushing open the door, she disappeared inside.

The two boys on the park bench looked at each other. Diggy was scowling.

"I should never have let her talk me into it," he

muttered. "It's too dangerous. What if he catches her?"

"She's the right person to do it," Sphinx answered. "She's a better actor than any of us, remember. Chessie can talk her way out of anything. And who's going to suspect a Girl Scout?"

Diggy nodded. "It was a good idea, I'll grant her that."

"It was an excellent idea," Sphinx said. "It was totally logical. I approve of that."

"You and your logic," snapped Diggy. "Tell me, what are we going to do if she gets into trouble—just sit here and wait for some kind of logical solution?"

□

Chessie walked slowly down the hall, her cookie boxes clutched in her arms, her Girl Scout hat perched neatly on top of her dark, glossy hair. She was scared to death. She would never have admitted it to the boys, not for a second, but she was really frightened. She had insisted on being the one to go; she had come up with the idea of dressing in her Girl Scout uniform. She had even convinced herself that the acting she had done for her father and Sergeant Gauss had whetted her appetite for this job. But now, as she walked down the hallway, she was not so sure. What if she couldn't even get near the computer room? Bobbie had shown her where it was, even drawn her a map, but what if she never made it past the receptionist? What if she fumbled, and they caught her trying to place the black box under the terminal? What would they do to her then? She had visions of being dragged up before Sergeant Gauss as a criminal . . . after she had smiled so sweetly at him and promised to stay out of trouble! No matter how things worked out, Chessie knew that she was *not* staying out of trouble. She was walking right into it.

The receptionist looked up and smiled as the pretty girl with long black hair came into the office, struggling with an armful of boxes.

"Hello," she said. "Let me guess what you're here for."

Chessie shifted the boxes and smiled at her, falling into her role.

"Hello," she replied, her voice high and childish (and innocent-sounding, too, she hoped). "I wonder—I wonder whether you'd like to buy any Girl Scout cookies?"

The receptionist glanced around her.

"Well, to tell you the truth, we're not supposed to accept any solicitations here."

Over the pile of cookie boxes Chessie looked at her mournfully. "It's for a good cause . . ." she ventured.

"Oh, I know, I know it is. It's just that I'm not supposed to. Office regulations, you know."

To her own surprise Chessie's dark eyes filled with tears.

"I've . . . I've got to sell a certain amount," she said, clutching the boxes to her. All this trouble, and now she couldn't even get past the receptionist!

"Oh, my goodness," sighed the woman, and, reaching beneath her desk, she took out her purse and counted out some money. "Oh, for goodness sake, don't cry. Let me see, what kinds of cookies are you selling? I guess I'll buy some for myself."

"Oh, thank you," cried Chessie. Dumping the boxes on the desk, she said, "These are peanut butter cookies . . . and here are the chocolate-filled kind . . . and these are mint-flavored . . . Do you like mint-flavored cookies?"

"Yes, that'll be fine," said the receptionist. "I'll take one box of those, and one of the chocolate-filled. That'll be fine. And now I think you'd better go, before Mr. Baring finds out."

"Thank you so much," said Chessie, gathering up the boxes into her arms. "These are just for demonstration, you know; they're actually for people who ordered them yesterday. I'll be back with yours tomorrow. And now, do you think there's anyone else here who might buy some cookies?"

The receptionist looked up, startled.

"Oh, no, no, you can't ask anyone else in this

office," she said quickly. "You can't . . . you can't . . . little girl! *Little girl!*"

It was too late. With the pile of cookies teetering precariously in her arms, Chessie headed for the corridor leading to Baring's private office and disappeared around the corner.

"Anybody want to buy some cookies?" she cried as she hurried down the hallway, aiming for the door to the computer room. She remembered Bobbie's instructions: the second door to the left.

The receptionist jumped up and rushed after her.

"Little girl!" she cried angrily. "Come back! Come back here!"

"I've got to sell a certain amount!" Chessie called over her shoulder. Stopping in front of the door, she managed to get her hand on the doorknob and twist it open.

She stumbled inside, the receptionist looming large behind her. With a shriek, she let go of her bundle of boxes, which flew haphazardly all over the room.

"Oh, my goodness," gasped Chessie, picking herself up and staring horrified all around her. "Oh, I'm so sorry. I'm so *sorry!*"

She had recognized the man sitting at the computer terminal as soon as the door had opened. From her friends' descriptions it could only be Baring himself.

"Oh, my goodness," choked Chessie, genuinely

horrified. She hadn't planned on bugging the terminal with Baring himself in the room! Quickly she began to rearrange her face into a smile.

"I'm sorry," she said. "I don't suppose—I don't suppose you'd like to buy some Girl Scout cookies?" She waved her hand at the boxes scattered all over the room. "An assortment," she continued, "all different kinds!"

Baring had half-risen from his chair as the girl tripped over the doorstep. Now he stared about at the pile of brightly wrapped packages and then turned a frigid stare on Chessie and the receptionist.

"Selma," he snapped, "what's going on here? Who is this girl?"

"I'm very sorry, Mr. Baring," said Selma, standing up with her arms full of boxes. "She came in trying to sell Girl Scout cookies and wouldn't take no for an answer. She ran in here before I could stop her."

Baring turned and stared at Chessie, who smiled back at him nervously.

"We have a quota," she explained, "of cookies to sell. And I thought if I could only talk to someone. . ."

"Just pick up the boxes and go," barked Baring. "And don't come back here again, okay? I have a strict rule in this office: no solicitors and no salesmen allowed, and that includes Girl Scouts—you get me?"

Chessie nodded, blushing, and Baring turned to the receptionist.

"I'm done in here," he said. "Selma, please help her out when she's finished. I'm going to see a client—I expect to be back around four o'clock."

"Yes, Mr. Baring."

He strode out. Selma glared at Chessie.

"That wasn't very nice," she said. "First I buy your cookies, and then you get me into trouble with my boss. Didn't your mother teach you any manners?"

"I'm sorry," Chessie said. "I feel terrible about it." In fact, she knew that her mother had had some trouble teaching her good manners.

She stooped by the terminal and began to gather up the boxes. Across the room Selma turned away and did the same.

Chessie paused by the terminal. She quickly reached into the pocket of her blouse, took out the small black box, and stuck it firmly to the underside of the console. Larry had shown her where to put it on the one at school. Then, crawling away on her hands and knees, she busied herself with clearing the floor. Some of the boxes had been torn or damaged in the fall, and she looked suitably woebegone as she picked them up.

"I don't know what I'll do," she said with a sigh. "I guess I'll just have to go back and start off with a new batch."

"Well, I hope you're more careful next time," Selma snapped. Rising to her feet, she dumped the boxes into Chessie's arms and followed her out of the room, turning out the lights and closing the door behind them.

Chessie headed obediently for the outer office. Once there, she turned around.

"I'm really sorry if I caused you any trouble. The last thing I wanted to do was to get you into hot water with your boss."

"Well, you did, anyway," Selma said, sitting down behind her desk. "I just don't understand why you had to go rushing off down there. But now scram, okay? Go bother someone else. I think there's a consulting firm next door that doesn't accept solicitations either. Why don't you try them?"

"Thanks," said Chessie. "I'll be back tomorrow with your cookies."

"Forget it, kid. You've gotten me into enough trouble. I don't want them anymore. I'm not doing you any favors."

Chessie's eyes grew wide.

"But you *promised*!" she said, coming up to the desk. "You *promised*!"

Selma sighed. "Don't start in with me!" she said. "You've been enough trouble as it is. Just get out of here, okay?"

"Look," said Chessie. "I promise I'll just bring the two boxes you ordered, and nothing else. Your boss won't even see me. I'll just drop your order off."

Selma shook her head. "You're persistent, I'll give you that," she said. "Okay. You bring the cookies, I'll pay for them, and then you'll leave . . . understood?"

Chessie nodded quickly.

"I was a Girl Scout once," Selma admitted. "Now leave me alone, okay?"

"See you tomorrow!" said Chessie, turning and heading for the front door. Once outside, she paused a moment, feeling the sudden wave of fear and relief. Then she headed off down the street, not even glancing at the park bench across from the office.

As she turned the corner Diggy and Sphinx looked at each other.

"She looks okay, doesn't she?" Sphinx muttered. "It must've worked."

"Hope so," said Diggy. "When will we know?"

"Tomorrow. I have third period free. If Baring is using his terminal during that time, I can get the password right away. Otherwise I'll have to wait until I have a chance to get back to the computer room."

They sat there for a while longer. After about a quarter of an hour, they stood up casually and strolled away, discussing the latest baseball scores and quarreling over Mike Schmidt's batting average.

5

☐ The next day a storm blew in and drenched the city. Lieutenant Commander Caldwell drove his son to school and let him off near the main entrance. Mumbling his thanks, Diggy made a dash for the door. During the trip he had been silent, staring out of the window, deliberately avoiding any conversation—about Annapolis in particular.

He was early for the history class. He slumped in his seat, staring moodily out of the window. All those puddles and wet leaves.

"What's up, sport?" Larry asked from across the aisle. "You look like you could chew iron. Or, as Ralph Waldo Emerson said—"

"So help me, Larry," Diggy snapped, "one more quote and I'll make you eat that book you get them from."

Larry stared. "Sorry, sport, I didn't know this was black Thursday. What's up?"

Diggy shook his head. "My father's after me about Annapolis again."

Larry whistled, and began to arrange his books on the desk. "Yeah, I know how it is. My family, too. They think I can't wait to be a rabbi, like my father and grandfather. They've got a surprise coming."

"Well, at least you can say that you don't have the calling."

Larry sighed. "Many are called, and few are Chosen People. Can you imagine me as a rabbi? The first electronic *rebbinu* at Beth Jacob? I suppose I could videotape my own sermons."

Diggy managed a smile.

"So why is your father in such a rush about Annapolis?" Larry asked. "You can't take the entrance exams for at least four years."

"I know, but they're starting a prep class at the Navy Yard, and my father wants me to go. That means giving up my weekends."

Larry shook his head. "That's tough."

"Yeah." Diggy slouched farther down in his seat. He had told his father that his school schedule was too heavy for him to take extra courses. His father understood that he would need top grades in school to apply to the Naval Academy, and, of course, he could always take the prep course next year. Diggy sighed, doodling in his notebook. The truth was, he did not want the Navy. He did not want to give up his weekends with the gang. Sphinx, Chessie, Bobbie, and Larry were his friends, and he had never been able to keep friends as his family moved from station to station. He needed them, and they needed him. How could his father expect him to give all that up for boring classes at the Navy Yard?

"Caldwell!" Mr. Houston's summons from the front of the class jerked Diggy from his thoughts. His head snapped away from the window, and he stared at the teacher.

"Yes, sir?"

"I was discussing the Conway Cabal. Would you care to give us your opinion of it?" Mr. Houston's voice sounded weary. "That is, of course, if you have one?"

During the summer Diggy had escaped reading the naval histories his father had given him by claiming to be absorbed in a large book on the American Revolution. Seeing him curled up in an alcove reading, his parents had left him alone. At first Diggy had flipped through the pages, half-asleep, but after a while he found himself reading about the battles and the political rivalry between the Continental Congress and the army. The Conway Cabal had been treated in detail.

"Well, sir, given the terrible condition of the

American army, the desertions, the mutinies, the defeats, General Conway thought that Congress should replace General Washington as commander-in-chief. Especially since General Gates was waiting to step in. What he failed to realize was that Congress was filled with Virginians, all friends of General Washington's, and all very touchy about the honor of Virginia. Since Congress was responsible for the sad state of the army—no pay, no money for food and equipment—they were too frightened of a split in their own ranks if they replaced Washington. General Conway was a fool."

There was muffled laughter in the class as Diggy finished. He had explained several points that Mr. Houston had not bothered to mention.

The teacher took it in good spirits. He thanked Diggy, made a note in his classbook, and continued his explanation of the events of 1777. Diggy listened for a while and then drifted off again into his own thoughts.

He was thinking about Sphinx. Would he get the account number and password? And then there was Chessie. Sure, she had been terrific in getting the box into Baring's office and hiding it under the terminal, but what now? She still had to go back to deliver the Girl Scout cookies and recover the damn thing. Suppose she got caught taking it off the terminal? Suppose she dropped it in front of everyone? Suppose the box hadn't worked at all?

But then who else could do the job? Chessie was the only one with an excuse to go into Baring's office. The receptionist was expecting her to come back. No, it had to be Chessie, but he didn't like the idea any better because of that.

He spent the rest of the class period worrying about his problems: his father, Sphinx, and Chessie. As far as he could see, there was no easy solution to any of them. The harsh ringing of the bell snapped him out of his musings. Gathering up his books, he fled to escape the good-natured joking of his classmates and the cries of "Cabal! Cabal!" that filled the room.

Diggy threaded his way through the corridors filled with chatting students. He passed the computer room, but it was only the second period. Too early for Sphinx. Chessie and Bobbie passed him, smiled, and gave him the thumbs-up salute of the Galaxy Gang. Diggy smiled, then hurried on to his next class. He spent a fretful hour in the physics lab timing a marble rolling down a plane. Math class was even worse. What was happening in the computer room?

As he walked into the lunchroom, he spotted Sphinx sitting alone at a table in the back, carefully unwrapping a ham and cheese sandwich. The other students usually left the lanky redhead alone—his conversation confused them. Sphinx had a habit of beginning a serious discussion, then sliding into double-talk without changing expression.

Diggy picked up his meal and sat down. "Hi."

"Hi."

"Did it work?"

Sphinx shook his head. "Nope. None of the print-outs showed any spaces between the letters. Probably Baring just hasn't been using his terminal."

"Either that," said Diggy, "or . . ."

"Or the pulser didn't work," finished Sphinx. He took a large bite of his sandwich. "I know. But I don't think that's it. Larry knows his stuff. If he says the thing will work, it'll work. The problem is getting to the school terminal at the same time that Baring's using his."

"Chessie is going back there after school, to take off the box."

"I know. Don't worry. Baring is sure to use it sometime this afternoon. I'll try again after lunch. If I have to, I'll skip physics and hide out in the computer room."

Diggy nodded. "Okay. Good luck, Sphinx."

The other boy drained his glass and stood up. "Mr. Henderson is sure going to think that I'm interested in this project," he said, strolling away. "So long."

□

Diggy went to his next class, where he messed up a French quiz. His mind was too far away for him to concentrate. When the bell rang, he hurried over to the computer room.

"Well?" he said.

Sphinx was sitting at the terminal. He was hunched over, his body a question mark. Even his hair looked frazzled.

"Go away," he said. "Leave me alone. There's nothing yet."

"I can't believe this," groaned Diggy. "I just failed a French quiz!"

"What about me?" asked Sphinx, quickly scanning a few pages of printout. "My teachers must be having a conference on where I am by now."

"Okay, look. Let me know when you get it, okay? I'll be in English class next."

"Great," said Sphinx. "Tell Mrs. Jenkins that I came down with a rare disease, and I won't be in today."

□

Diggy was walking out of English class when he saw Sphinx coming down the hall, waving a piece of paper. He looked triumphant.

"Eureka!" he said. "Look at this."

He handed Diggy the slip of paper. There was a string of numbers and then one word carefully printed on it: OSCAR.

"Can you believe it?" Sphinx said. "He uses his own first name for the password. I probably could have guessed it without all this trouble. Shows what a creative mind he has."

"Or what a short memory," Diggy said, pocketing the slip. "Good work, Sphinx."

"So Chessie'll go back to Baring's office today?"

Diggy nodded, slowly. It was clear he hated the idea.

Sphinx looked at him. "Don't change the plan," he advised. "You know Chessie. She'll think it's a male chauvinistic piggy thing. And you know what? She'd be right."

□

"Aren't you afraid?" Bobbie asked. She was sitting on the edge of the bed, her feet tucked under her, eating an orange and watching Chessie change into her Girl Scout uniform. They had come straight to the Morelli house from school and locked themselves into Chessie's bedroom. They often did their homework together, and Bobbie was considered one of the family.

Chessie straightened the kerchief and smoothed back her glossy black hair. She stared into the mirror.

"Gosh, I don't know, Bobbie. Maybe it's because I was brought up in South Philly. You can't imagine what went on in that neighborhood. I couldn't let the boys see that I was scared, 'cause then they'd be after me all the time. And I had to learn to fight too, because there's none of that Italian gallantry toward women you hear about—not around there, anyway. So I got used to it. Sometimes I was really scared . . . but at least nobody knew!"

Bobbie nodded. She herself was too tall and too good at karate to have been bothered that way. In fact, she often worried that boys paid too little attention to her.

"What will you do if Baring finds out what you're there for?" she asked.

Chessie straightened her skirt and tilted her cap, arranging it carefully. "Oh, I can handle him." But her heart was pounding.

Ten minutes later they left the house and walked toward Baring's office, five blocks away. On the corner they separated. Bobbie promised to wait for her in the little park where Sphinx and Larry would be waiting until Chessie arrived safely with the black box. "And I wouldn't be surprised to find Diggy on the scene either," Bobbie said. She smiled mischievously at the blush on Chessie's face. She knew that Diggy Caldwell was the one boy Chessie really liked.

"See you!" Chessie said, turning the corner.

□

"Remember me?" Chessie smiled as she held up the boxes of cookies.

Selma groaned and looked furtively around the office. "Oh, yes, I remember. You could have gotten me fired. Let me have the cookies, and then please go. If my boss sees you again . . ."

"I'm sorry about yesterday. I didn't mean to make trouble for you. Let's see, you ordered one box of mint and one of chocolate-filled."

Chessie examined the boxes carefully, reading the labels, and making certain there were no rips in the wrapping while Selma fidgeted.

"Okay, here they are," Chessie said. "Thank you very much."

"Here's the money. Good-bye."

"Good-bye." Chessie turned to go, and then stopped, a woeful look on her face. "Gosh, I hate to be such a nuisance, but last time I think I dropped an earring back there when we were picking up the boxes." She pointed to the single earring in her left ear. "It looks like that. You see, it means a lot to me because they were my grandmother's. Could we just take a quick look?"

Selma stared at her. "You want to look around the room you were in yesterday?"

"Yes, that's right. I'm sorry, but I can't imagine where else it could be."

"Oh, well. Come with me."

Chessie followed her down the hallway. She was very pleased with herself. This had turned out to be easier than she had thought.

"This is the room," said Selma, opening the door.

"Why don't you look over there and I'll search the floor here."

On their hands and knees they felt into all the dark spots under the desks, around the edges of the rug, and around the filing cabinets. The woman turned her back on Chessie for a moment to look under the copier. Quickly Chessie reached underneath the console. Her hand touched only the smooth metal surface. She slid her hand from side to side. Nothing! Frantically, she reached from front to back. She *knew* that she had put the box just under the front edge of the terminal . . . but now it was gone. Could it have fallen off? No, it would have been found and then. . . .

As Chessie groped on her hands and knees, she was suddenly aware of a man's black shoes next to her. She looked up.

Baring stared down at her, his face a cold mask, the black box in the palm of his hand. "Is this what you're looking for, young lady?"

Chessie stared up at him, her mouth open. She tried to speak, but her voice was a harsh croak. She glanced over at the secretary, her eyes pleading, but her hopes were shattered by Baring's next words.

"All right, Selma. Nice going. All we had to do was wait. And now look who's walked into our trap." He glanced down at Chessie. "Selma didn't believe that a twelve-year-old Girl Scout would try to bug our computer. Neither did I . . . until right now. Okay, Selma, you can go back to your desk."

He waited until the receptionist was gone. "This gadget was messing up the computer, kid. We called a repairman, and he found it this afternoon."

Hard to run when you're on your hands and knees, Chessie thought, glancing at the door.

"Get up!" Baring's voice was brutal. "You've got some talking to do."

Chessie rose slowly, brushing off her skirt. She faced Baring boldly and opened her mouth as if to say something. Then, quickly, she ducked and bolted for the door.

She was almost there when Baring grabbed her from behind. She twisted away and slammed into the edge of a filing cabinet. A sharp pain ran through her right shoulder and down her side. She slid to the floor and bit her lip to keep from crying.

The voice above her seemed far away as she tried to get off the floor. Her side ached terribly. All she could think of was Sergeant Gauss's warning that Baring could well be a dangerous man.

Diggy stood up, his eyes fixed on the sign above Baring's door. "No time to call the police. Besides, what could we tell them—that Chessie is in there selling Girl Scout cookies and we think she may be in trouble? They'd just laugh."

"But she may be in trouble," said Bobbie.

"Sphinx, what do you think?" asked Diggy.

Sphinx frowned, rocking back on his heels. His elbows stuck out of the holes in his faded blue sweater. He stared across the street at the office door.

"There's no choice," he said. "We'll have to go in ourselves, and right now. I didn't like the way Phillips looked when he came out."

"Okay," said Diggy. "All four of us, together. Let's go."

□

Selma glanced up as the four teenagers came down the hallway.

"Hi," said Bobbie, smiling. "Remember me and my brother?" She indicated Sphinx.

"Yes, I remember you," said the woman. "What are you doing here? Who are these other kids?"

"These are some friends of ours," Bobbie said. "They decided to come along."

"Well, you have no business here," snapped Selma.

"Oh, but we do," said Sphinx. "We're looking for our Uncle Herbie. He told us to meet him here."

6

□ "What's your name?"

Looking up, Chessie saw Baring towering over her.

"What's your name?" he growled. Behind him, the door opened.

"C'mon, kid, you've got a few questions to answer," said Baring. He pulled her to her feet and shook her roughly.

From behind him came a man's worried voice. "Don't hurt her. What are you going to do?"

"Shut up, Phillips!" Baring turned and shoved Chessie into a chair.

The other man moved around to stand next to his boss. Phillips was a small, thin man with dark hair and a mustache. Chessie glanced around in despair.

"How could a kid her age be involved in this?" asked Phillips.

"Shut up!" said Baring. "There have been just too many kids around this office lately." He leaned forward, staring at Chessie grimly.

"Listen to me, kiddo," he said. "I don't know what you're up to, but it's gonna get you into big trouble—you know what I mean?"

Chessie gazed at him and her eyes filled with tears.

"So I want your name. I want you to tell me what this little black box is and why you put it there. Okay?"

Chessie shook her head stubbornly.

Baring scowled. "You'd better talk, and fast! Do you hear me?"

"I don't know what you mean," wailed Chessie. "I don't know anything! I just wanted to sell some cookies!"

"I've had it with that stupid story!" Baring cried. Grabbing Chessie by the shoulders, he shook her furiously.

Phillips made a sudden move forward.

"Stop . . . stop it!" he cried. "What are you doing? Stop it!"

"Now tell me the truth!" yelled Baring. Hauling Chessie to her feet, he slapped her smartly across the face. She shrank away and turned pale. Phillips

backed off across the room, his hands waving n vously in the air.

"I . . . I'm not going to have anything to do w. this," he stammered. "Nothing! Do you hear? Not ing!" And, turning, he was gone. The door close with a sharp click behind him.

Baring turned back to Chessie.

"Okay," he said, "now you're going to give m some answers."

□

"Diggy, look!" cried Bobbie.

Diggy followed her gaze. Sphinx came up beside them, and Larry stopped his pacing to watch.

Across the street, the door to Baring's office had just opened. Out stumbled a small, thin, dark-haired man who looked around and then dashed off down the street.

"That's Phillips!" said Bobbie.

"You're sure?" asked Diggy.

"Of course I'm sure. I saw him in the office, didn't I? That's him, all right. He looks like a fiel mouse."

"Something's happened," said Larry. "Son thing's gone wrong. It's been too long."

Diggy nodded and glanced at his watch.

"She should have been out fifteen minutes he said.

"What are we going to do?" asked Bobbie

The woman stared at him coldly.

"I'm sorry, but we're not seeing any clients today," she said. "I'm afraid your uncle was mistaken. You'll just have to wait for him somewhere else."

Sphinx glanced at Bobbie.

"Oh, no," he said earnestly, "Uncle Herbie never makes mistakes like that. I'm sure he said this office."

"Me, too," chimed in Bobbie.

"Well, you'll have to wait for him outside then. Now get out of here!"

Sphinx shook his head. "When Uncle Herbie says here, he means *here*—" he started to explain. All at once from the back office they heard a man's voice raised in anger.

Diggy was around the corner and pelting down the hallway before Selma could make a move.

Diggy knew where the computer room was from Bobbie's description. He reached the door and yanked it wide open.

"I don't *know* what it is!" Chessie was shrieking, her face streaked with tears. "For the hundredth time, I don't know! *Let me go!*"

Baring was standing in front of her, the pulser in his outstretched hand. As the four kids tumbled in, followed by Selma, he whirled and shoved the box into his pocket.

"Selma! What's this? What's going on?"

"I'm sorry, Mr. Baring," said Selma. "They just ran in here before I could stop them."

Baring's glance was fixed on Bobbie's face.

"You!" he barked. "What are you doing here?"

"Why, waiting for my uncle," Bobbie said primly. "Then I thought I heard a scream. Are you all right?" she asked Chessie.

Chessie nodded through her tears.

"Hey," said Larry, "don't I know you? You're from our school, aren't you?" He came up beside her. "What's he been doing to you?"

"I just came in to . . . to sell some cookies," Chessie sobbed, "and this man started shouting at me and shaking me and talking about this crazy black box. I don't know anything about that! I just wanted to sell some cookies!"

Baring and Selma glanced at each other. Diggy scowled. "What's going on here? Maybe I should call the police."

"I don't have to explain myself to a bunch of kids," Baring shouted. "Get out of my office!"

"Thanks, we will," replied Diggy and, taking Chessie's hand, he led her to the door.

"Not that one! I haven't finished questioning her yet!"

Diggy pushed Chessie through the door and the four teenagers turned to face Baring.

"I think you *have* finished questioning her," said

Diggy. "She's coming with us, or else I'll call the police."

"About what? I haven't done anything," Baring began. From behind the kids a high-pitched voice broke in.

"The *police*?" The gang turned to see Phillips standing in the hallway, staring at them. "The police?"

"C'mon," Bobbie whispered to Chessie. Brushing past the trembling clerk, they hurried toward the lobby.

"What are all these kids doing here?" Phillips was asking as the three boys turned to leave.

Diggy wheeled around. Planting himself in front of Phillips, he looked him squarely in the eye and said, "The father of that girl has friends in the police department, and you can be sure that they'll hear about this . . . *soon*!"

Phillips paled, and glanced at his boss.

"Get out of here!" shouted Baring. "What do you have to tell the police? Nothing! Get out of my office!"

"Okay," said Diggy. He and the other boys headed for the exit. As they left, Sphinx lagged behind to call over his shoulder at Selma, "By the way . . . in case my Uncle Herbie does show up— please tell him we waited for as long as we could!"

7

☐ "Yes, Diggy," Judge Jarre⬚⬚⬚ "that's a puzzle." He leaned back in ⬚⬚⬚ ir and stared thoughtfully across the desk. Diggy had just finished the story about Baring, the Xuans, and how the Galaxy Gang had gotten the all-important password. Several times the judge had looked disapproving, but once or twice the corners of his mouth had turned up in a slight smile.

The judge thought it over in silence. They were sitting in his study, a small, sparsely furnished back room lined with bookshelves. The only sound was the ticking of a clock on the mantel, but to Diggy the noise was deafening. As he waited for the judge's verdict the pounding of his heart seemed to reinforce the ticking. His face felt flushed.

"An interesting case," the judge said finally.

"Something new in my experience, what with the computers and all that. Still, I suppose the existing law that governs personal privacy, trade secrets, the confidentiality of corporate records, and, of course, unlawful entry, applies here."

Diggy's heart sank as the judge ticked off the list.

"Fortunately," the judge continued, "there's been no overt act—as yet. There's been no actual violation of the confidentiality of private records, no wrongful appropriation of funds or proprietary information. . ."

"Sir," Diggy interrupted, "that man is a crook and, so far, the law hasn't been able to touch him. You mean to say that the only way he can be caught is by breaking the law?"

"Diggy, please understand that the law is not perfect. It's just the best set of rules we know of to deal with the problems of a society. When our ancestors crawled out of the caves and began living together in tribes and later in villages, they made rules to govern people's behavior. Over the centuries the first simple rules became more complicated, grew into many rules covering almost all aspects of life. The law tells us that you can't steal from someone else, or strike him, or threaten to do him harm. And, most important, it tells us our rights: the security of our homes and of our persons, free speech, protection against unlawful arrest and imprisonment."

The judge leaned forward and pointed a finger at Diggy. "And it protects our private papers, too. This man, Baring, has not been convicted of any crime. He is entitled to be considered innocent until a jury finds him guilty. Until then, he is guaranteed the full protection of the law—including the security and confidentiality of his business records. If anyone tampers with those records in any way, that would be no different from breaking into Baring's safe. It would be a violation of the law, and the penalties are very severe indeed."

Diggy stared out of the large window behind the desk. There was a tiny garden there, the judge's delight. The light of early evening was fading fast, and deep shadows were gathering under the yews and along the picket fence.

"Suppose we give the information to the police and told them how we got it?" the boy asked.

Judge Jarrell frowned and shook his head. "Tainted evidence, Diggy. Any court would throw out evidence obtained that way. You can't prove that a crime has been committed with evidence obtained illegally."

Diggy nodded. "Yes, sir, I understand. I also understand that the law forbids us to obtain the proof of Baring's swindles."

"To do that, you'd have to become as guilty as you say this man Baring is."

"He *is* guilty! He stole Mr. Xuan's . . ."

"No, Diggy. You *say* he's a crook and that he stole Mr. Xuan's money, but until that's been proven, Baring's rights will be protected by the same law that protects your rights and mine."

"Then there's nothing that can be done?"

The judge fumbled with some papers on his desk. There was a long silence.

"Well," he said at last, "of course, there *is* one person who can give evidence."

Diggy sat up. "Who's that, sir?"

"Baring. Or anyone else who knows what he's doing."

Diggy stared at him. "I don't understand. Baring won't help prove he's a crook. Why should he?"

The judge smiled. "I didn't say that he would, did I? But I also said something about another person who is involved. And that is *all* that I can say, my boy. As your legal advisor, I've warned you not to go ahead with your plan. Remember, I'm still a judge. If I thought you were about to do something criminal, I'd have to tell the police."

The judge cleared his throat, and twisted a pencil in his hands. "Yes, there seems to be another person involved. Shouldn't be surprised if he were rather nervous about this whole business. He'd be even more frightened if he knew how close you were to putting him in jail."

□

After dinner, Diggy volunteered to do the dishes—alone. His mother gave him a surprised look, then nodded. He was scrubbing the pots and pans when his parents stuck their heads into the kitchen to say good-bye. They were spending the evening at a concert.

As soon as he heard the front door close, Diggy wiped his hands, picked up the telephone, and dialed Sphinx's number. He shifted from foot to foot as the phone rang and rang at the other end. The Osgoods must be out for the evening, too. Sphinx was either with them or at the library.

Quickly finishing his chores, Diggy grabbed a jacket and nearly ran the four blocks to the ivy-covered local branch of the Free Library. He knew exactly where to look for his friend: deep in the stacks where the science and math books were. Sure enough, there was Sphinx sprawled on the floor, reading and munching on an apple. Only Sphinx could get away with eating in the library—he had made a point of being friendly to the librarian.

"I would think she'd let you eat a five-course dinner in here by now," Diggy said, sitting down next to him. He glanced at the spine of the book which had Sphinx so absorbed. *Men of Mathematics*—well, that figured.

"I talked to the judge," Diggy continued. Sphinx

closed his book. Then he rolled over onto his back and smiled.

"Shall I tell you what His Honor said? He told you that we're about to commit a terrible crime and warned you what's going to happen to us. Being boiled alive in oil, for instance, or beheaded. Well, of *course* that's what he'd say. He doesn't know Tilo and the Xuans and how important it is for us to stop Baring. All he knows is that the law says we're about to become desperate criminals." Sphinx took a last bite of his apple, and shoved the core into his pants pocket.

Diggy nodded. He was not surprised that Sphinx had guessed right. Besides, he suspected that Sphinx had already checked the lawbooks in the library already.

"So what do we do?" Sphinx asked. "Do we quit, or do it anyway and throw ourselves on the mercy of the court?"

Diggy glanced around. "We haven't committed a crime until we go into Baring's records, right?"

Puzzled, Sphinx scratched his cheek. "Right."

"Okay, then, I have an idea how we can get what we want without going any further. The judge started me thinking about it."

Sphinx's gaze shifted from the ceiling to Diggy's face. "Okay, so tell me!"

"Nope." Diggy grinned and got to his feet. "I

haven't thought it out yet. There's something I want to discuss with Tilo first. Anyway, it'll give you something to think about when you're bored with *Men of Mathematics*."

Sphinx's eyes were slowly starting to glaze. "It *is* an interesting problem," he mumbled.

"So long!"

□

The next morning when Tilo came down from the apartment above the tailor shop he was surprised to find Diggy waiting for him.

"I thought we could walk to school together," Diggy said. "I need some advice, Tilo."

The two boys walked down the street lined with shops and turned the corner. They came to the new embankment above the express highway that skirted the Delaware River and strolled along it, watching the cars speed by and the freighters move slowly through the dark water. To Tilo, the heavy traffic was a constant surprise. "So many cars," he marveled. "In our village I saw maybe two or three trucks a year, and everyone came out to touch them."

Diggy pointed out an oil tanker moving away from a refinery dock. "She's taking on water, for ballast, you know. So she won't roll as much in heavy seas." He went on to explain how important is was to have the weight just right in a big ship. "In one typhoon in the Pacific, the Navy lost three destroyers. They just turned over because their fuel tanks were almost empty."

"You know so much about ships. Do you think of being an officer in the Navy?"

Diggy looked sharply at the Vietnamese boy. Had someone told him about Annapolis? Probably, since the whole gang knew about it.

"No," he said, "I don't want a career in the Navy. It's too tough. My father was gone for months at a time on sea duty. I really missed him. Sure, my mother did what she could, but I never got to know my father." Tilo nodded sympathetically.

"Besides," said Diggy, "there are things I want to study, things I want to learn about instead of ships and engines."

"Like what?"

"I'm not sure yet. Maybe politics or history. I'm really into military history these days."

Tilo looked sad. "Yes, we Vietnamese know a lot about military history. We saw so much of it."

Diggy flushed. "Look, Tilo, that's what I wanted to talk to you about—but if it's too painful, let's just drop it."

"No, it's okay. I can talk about it. Others can't . . . but I can."

"Okay, here it is. We were in Japan during the Vietnam War. My father was stationed at Osaka naval headquarters. Lots of his friends are Army men, and they used to visit us and talk about the

Vietcong. They said the VC had very clever ways of making the villagers pay a tax to support the rebellion. Even the reluctant ones were scared into giving money and food. How was that done?"

They had reached the square in front of the school. Tilo glanced around, and then pulled Diggy to one side and spoke in a low, rapid voice. "They would come late at night, every night for a week, two weeks, even longer. If there was a man who did not want to pay the tax, they would go to his house and blow a bugle. Just one long, loud call. Then they would go away until the next night. There was no one the man could go to for help. Everyone was afraid. So every night he would wait without sleep for that one bugle sound. Sooner or later he would pay, just to get some sleep."

"Did anyone refuse to pay?"

"In my village only one man. He went mad, and they took him away to the hospital in Saigon. We never saw him again." Tilo paused. "This is not a Vietnamese invention, you know, Diggy. Our old enemies, the Chinese, first thought it up. It's only a new form of the water-drop torture they used for centuries."

□

"The Chinese water-drop torture," Diggy wrote in his notebook, "was used for hundreds of years to make criminals talk. The victim was tied so that he could not move his head, then drops of water fell on his skull at a never-changing rate of one per second. In a week the victim was babbling, eager to talk and confess. Anything to stop the monotonous splash of drops on his head."

He drew a large circle about the paragraph and read it several times. In front of the class, Mr. Houston was explaining the events that led to the British surrender at Yorktown. The teacher eyed Diggy, but decided not to call on him. The Conway Cabal incident had made him cautious.

Underneath the circled paragraph, Diggy wrote one word in large capitals: PHILLIPS. Then he closed the notebook and looked up. Across the room a worried Chessie was watching him. He smiled at her. By now she must have heard from Sphinx what had happened in the library, and about the idea Diggy would not reveal. He had decided to keep his plan to himself for a little while longer. If it turned out to be a disaster, let it be his responsibility. He still felt guilty about the way Baring had treated Chessie. No more of that if he could help it.

When the period bell rang, Diggy gathered his books and hurried down the hall to the telephone. There was only one Samuel T. Phillips in the directory. He scribbled the address and telephone number on a slip of paper and put it in his wallet. Soon the Chinese water torture would begin—drip, drip, drip on Phillips's head. Would it take a week? Probably not. The guy was nervous now, and it should not take much to get him to talk. Diggy slipped his wallet into his back pocket and hurried off down the hall.

Tonight the first bugle call would sound.

□

Diggy was halfway through his homework when his mother came into his room with an armful of laundry. He knew that something was troubling her from the way she began to put things away without a word. Her back was stiff, and she had a disapproving way of dropping his shirts into the drawers. Neither of them spoke.

When she was done putting his clothes away, she came over to the desk. He looked up from his books and waited.

"You've decided that you don't want Annapolis, haven't you, Diggy?" Her low voice held a hint of strain.

Diggy nodded and fumbled with his pencil. "Gosh, Mom, I never wanted it. Dad never asked me if I wanted the Navy as a career. He just assumed that I would because that's what he wants for me. It's not fair. I have the right to make up my own mind."

"Please understand, Diggy. Your father loves you very much and would never force you to do anything. It's just that the Navy is his whole life—except for us—and it's only natural that he'd want his son to follow him. Tradition is important to Navy men."

"Listen, Mom, Dad's people were farmers in Vermont. There's not exactly a long tradition of Navy men in our family."

"Your father hoped to be the beginning of one."

"I'm sorry."

Mrs. Caldwell picked up a book from the floor and put it on the desk. "I understand, Diggy. But you owe it to your father to tell him how you feel."

Diggy nodded.

His mother took his face in her hands and smiled down at him. Then she kissed his forehead and left. She closed the door quietly, leaving Diggy staring at his work.

□

Late that night, when the house was silent, Diggy tiptoed down to the kitchen, a small flashlight in his hand. He found a roll of aluminum foil under the sink and tore off a piece, carefully crumpling it. The slip of paper was in the pocket of his bathrobe. He took it out and stared at it, then dialed slowly. The phone at the other end rang three times before a sleepy voice answered.

"Hello?"

Diggy placed the crumpled foil over the mouthpiece and ran his thumb over it. There was a sharp crackling, magnified by the voice box, that gave the impression of a long-distance call. Diggy knew that the foil would also deepen and disguise his voice, making it sound older, more threatening.

"Phillips?"

"Yes? Who is this? What's the idea of calling me at this hour?"

"Just listen, Phillips. I'm going to do you a big favor. They're going to grab Baring any day now. They'll get you, too, if you're not smart. They've cracked your little scheme."

The voice on the other end was a frightened squawk now. "What? Who is this? What do you mean by—"

"Just listen. They know all about that dummy corporation, and they've got the account number and the password for the computer. I'm telling you, any day now they're going to crack down."

Diggy hung up before the man could answer. He threw the aluminum foil into the trashcan, went to the refrigerator and poured himself a glass of milk. As he drank it he thought of Phillips sitting in the darkness of his bedroom, telephone in hand, wondering.

Drip. The first drop of water had fallen on Phillips's head.

Would it take a week? Diggy thought not.

He drained his glass, washed it out, and went back to bed.

8

☐ The next day, after his last class, Diggy hurried outside. There, leaning against the flagpole was Sphinx, a sandwich in his hand. This was his mid-to-late afternoon snack, right before his pre-dinner snack.

"Hi," said Diggy, coming up to him.

Sphinx waved the sandwich in greeting. He was wearing a purple shirt whose sleeves were too short for him, leaving his bony wrists sticking out. He wore, as always, his ancient jeans ("Had them since the Ice Age," he would say fondly) and worn red sneakers. Today a large gray woolen scarf was tied loosely around his neck, and his hair looked as if it had been combed with a rake.

"Well, Mr. Spock," Diggy said, "did you figure

out how we can nail Baring without breaking the law?"

Sphinx smiled.

"Perhaps," he said. "And then again, perhaps not." He took a gigantic bite of his sandwich and lounged back against the flagpole.

Diggy leaned toward him.

"Sphinx," he said, "you're bluffing. If you know, let's hear it."

"Now, now," Sphinx said mildly. He brushed the bread crumbs off his jacket and sighed. "Okay," he said, "but there's just one condition."

"And what's that?"

"If I guess right, you buy me an ice cream sundae with all the trimmings."

Diggy grinned. "And if you guess wrong? Never mind, it's a deal."

Sphinx closed his eyes.

"Here are the facts," he said. "You have the password, but you won't use it because that's illegal. Also, you don't intend to quit. The judge told you that any proof we get illegally is no proof at all. Yet it's clear you're going to use the password somehow. That is the puzzle."

He paused, opening his eyes and squinting into the sun.

"That's the puzzle," he repeated. Beside him Diggy squirmed impatiently. "Okay," Sphinx continued, "you obviously intend to use the password itself . . . but *not* to break into Baring's records. Do you plan to trick Baring into confessing by telling him you have 'Oscar'? No way. He won't scare. He'll just change the password. No, that's not the answer."

"You're close, though," said Diggy. "I'm afraid your time is up."

"No time limit," Sphinx announced. "No time limit. Now where was I? The receptionist and that guy Josephson probably don't know the password. Who else is there, then?" He gazed at Diggy. "The clerk," he said. "Phillips. You're going to scare him into confessing?"

Diggy blinked. Sphinx's logic was impressive.

"Right on the first guess," he said. "Okay, so you win the car and the trip to Hawaii. Or would you prefer what's behind Door Number One?"

"Oh, the door, the door," said Sphinx. "I always go for the big money. What's behind Door Number One?"

"A punch in the mouth," said Diggy.

"Oh, forget it, I'll take the car and the vacation," said Sphinx. "What a waste. I thought I'd win a million dollars."

"Never mind. What does 'all the trimmings' mean?"

Sphinx grinned at him. "You'll find out!"

□

It was two A.M.

The phone rang, and the man reached out from his sleep, fumbling for it.

"Hello? Who is this?"

"Hello, Phillips. It's me again," said the voice, muffled by the long-distance static.

"Who . . . what?"

"A friend of yours, Phillips. A good friend. Now listen. They're getting closer. Baring's in real hot water. They know the kind of fishy deals he's been involved in. They know where all that money went. Do you hear me, Phillips?"

The man opened his mouth in the darkness, but nothing came out except a terrified croak.

"You said it," said the voice. "You're just lucky that you've got a friend in me. If I were you, Phillips, I'd get out of this, and fast. You understand?"

"No . . . no," gasped the man.

There was a sharp click, and the line went dead.

Miles away, Diggy stared at the phone he had just placed back on the hook. There was a thoughtful look on his face.

Drip, drip, drip, he said to himself.

□

Sphinx had advised Diggy not to use the password right away in his phone conversation with Phillips.

"Wait till he's about to crack," he said. Diggy had agreed.

The next day they held a short meeting in the

school lunchroom. Everyone was there, including Tilo.

"I want to know what's going on," said Chessie indignantly.

"It's not fair," Larry put in. "Here we do all this work, and then all of a sudden we're not included in the plans. 'The used key is always bright.' Benjamin Franklin. 'We're in this together, Robin.' " He looked around the table. "Batman, I think."

"I had hoped," Tilo said timidly, "that I could help. All this is for my family. It's only right that some of the risk be mine."

"Okay, okay," said Diggy. "I didn't want to talk about it because after that scare with Baring and Chessie I thought it'd be better for just one of us to go on with it alone. I went to Judge Jarrell and gave him the final say on whether we should go ahead."

"What did he tell you?" asked Bobbie.

"That it was strictly illegal, and we'd get nowhere with it," said Diggy.

There was silence. Tilo stared down at his hands.

"But," Diggy said quickly, "there's another way, and the judge gave me a hint what it could be. Listen."

He told them about the late-night calls. Then he leaned back and yawned. "And don't think that it's easy to get up at six for school when you've been up till two."

"Please," said Tilo, "I want to help. I want to call Phillips myself."

"No," put in Sphinx. "It's not a good idea. Phillips will know it's not the same voice."

Diggy hesitated.

"Well," he said, "I'm not so sure about that. The tinfoil over the mouthpiece disguises my voice completely. And Phillips is so scared, he probably wouldn't even notice."

"Please," said the Vietnamese boy. "I want to do it. I know I can."

"Phillips is frightened," Diggy said. "The next call is going to be the last one. Whoever does it will have to get it just right. You'll have to mention the password, and drop the hint about confessing at the same time."

"I can do it," said Tilo. "I know I can."

Diggy glanced around the table. The others were nodding.

"Okay," he said. "It seems fair to me. It was Tilo's idea to try the Chinese water trick, after all. Let Tilo finish him off!"

□

"Is there something wrong, my son?" Mrs. Xuan regarded Tilo with worried eyes.

"No, mama," murmured the boy. He was sitting at dinner and toying listlessly with his food.

Mrs. Xuan stood up and began to clear away the

dishes, her eyes still on her son. She said nothing, but she knew him too well. Her gaze made Tilo even more nervous. Standing up, he announced, "I'm going to my room to do some homework."

His older sister, Kim, cocked her head at him and laughed. "What, suddenly a scholar!" she teased.

They were speaking in Vietnamese, although Kim had tried to insist on English being spoken in the home. She wanted very badly for her parents to stop being so "old-fashioned" and to join this exciting new world. But at home it was too easy to slip back into their familiar language.

The baby, Won, Tilo's younger brother, waved his spoon in the air and gurgled happily as food splattered all around. Mrs. Xuan scolded, laughing, as she picked him up.

"May I go?" asked Tilo, wavering.

"Yes, go ahead," said his father. "Do your work, son. Don't laugh at him, Kim—it's important to work hard."

Tilo went to his room and sat down on his bed. Do your work, work hard . . . that was all his father had to say to him these days. Didn't he understand how difficult it was for him to talk in class? He was learning rapidly, but he was still not at home in his adopted language. He was happy about one thing, however: he could understand the detective programs and western movies on TV on Saturday afternoon. He watched them every week, sitting wide-eyed and fascinated for hours.

His mother teased him about becoming so American. His father never spoke to him about it, as if he were unhappy at the thought of his son losing his ties to their native country.

It was the excitement of the chase, the same feeling of danger, that he liked about Diggy's plan for dealing with Phillips. That afternoon, after school, he and Diggy had carefully gone over what he would say on the phone. Now it was up to him to carry it through.

Downstairs, Kim took the baby into the living room while his parents, with tired faces, sat and talked in the kitchen. They had done this every night since his father's savings had vanished. They still had not recovered from the shock. They sat and talked, wearily trying to make plans for their future.

□

1:30 A.M. A phone was ringing.

"Hello?"

"Hello, Phillips," said Tilo. He was sitting downstairs in the kitchen, the phone cupped in his hands, his voice low. "It's me again. Your friend, remember?"

There was a pause.

"Listen," said the man. "Why are you doing this?"

"You listen," said Tilo briskly. "They're about to grab your boss. They know everything now. The dummy corporation, hiding the cash, everything. Do you want to go to jail with Baring?"

"I don't believe you!" cried the clerk. "If it's true, why would you be calling me up like this? What information could they have?" He stopped, abruptly. "We . . . we haven't done anything," he stammered. "You're just trying to smear me and my boss!"

"Phillips, don't be a fool. Get out while you still can. If you confess now, they'll go easy on you."

"You have no proof . . . nothing! How do I know that this isn't just a bunch of lies you've cooked up to scare me?"

Tilo gripped the phone. This was the moment.

"Phillips," he said, "let me ask you just one thing. Does the word 'Oscar' mean anything to you . . . besides being your boss's first name?"

There was silence on the other end of the line. Tilo ran his finger over the tinfoil covering the mouthpiece.

"You see?" he said. "I can't say any more. But if I were you, I'd spill the beans. The jig is up."

Click.

Tilo stared doubtfully at the phone. Were "spill

the beans" and "the jig is up" the right words, or had he mixed up his slang?

□

"I think you did a great job," said Diggy. He had listened carefully to Tilo's account of the previous night's phone call, and now he leaned back in his chair and nodded. "Sounds perfect, Tilo."

"I think I said it correctly," the other boy said nervously. "I spent the whole evening in my room, planning what to say. I'm sure he didn't notice that it wasn't the same person."

"Sounds good," said Bobbie. The gang had gathered again in the lunchroom to hear Tilo's story. "So what do we do now?"

"Now?" asked Diggy. He leaned forward and glanced over at Sphinx.

"Yeah," said Larry. "Do you want any more information? We could use the password to get into that account and find out the name of the dummy corporation that Baring's using to cover his extra cash."

"Illegal," said Sphinx.

"Even if we don't print out any of the money transfers?" said Larry.

Diggy shook his head.

"So far we haven't broken into the files at all," he said. "We have the account number and password, but we haven't used them on the computer. And that's how it's going to stay."

"Are you going to check up on Phillips?" asked Chessie. "Maybe give him just one more call?"

"Nope," said Diggy, grinning at her. "That's it."

"That's it?" echoed Chessie, disappointed.

"Sorry, but that's all we can do. Maybe later on we'll try one more call, if we don't have him rattled enough already—but I think we should just stop and wait. Give him time to think it over. Give him time to build up to a real panic."

"Okay," said Sphinx, tilting back his chair and gulping down his milkshake. "So, we wait?"

"That's right."

" 'Everything comes,' " Larry pronounced solemnly, " 'if a man will only wait.' Benjamin Disraeli."

□

The days crawled by. Every afternoon Diggy asked Chessie, "Have you heard?"

She shook her head.

"Sergeant Gauss came by," she said one day, "but only on a social visit. Don't worry," she added hastily when she saw Diggy's face, "we'll be the first to hear if Phillips turns himself in. Sergeant Gauss knows I'm interested in the case."

A few days later Tilo asked, "Do you think perhaps we should call again?"

"No, I still don't think so," said Diggy. "I'm sure he's mulling it over. If we look too eager, he might back off from the whole thing. We'll just have to wait and see."

□

A week after Tilo's phone call Chessie was on her way home from school when she heard a familiar bellow behind her. Turning, she waved as Sergeant Gauss's battered Camaro pulled up beside her.

"Francesca!" he roared, sticking his head out of the window. "Time for lasagna!"

"C'mon, Sergeant, I made you lasagna only a few weeks ago," laughed Chessie. "What is it now?"

The burly police officer glanced around.

"You know that guy Baring you're so interested in?" he said. "Well, I can't say I had anything to do with it, but it seems that his clerk turned himself in to the D.A. just a few hours ago. Confessed everything. The guy really had quite a business going . . . a real high-level operation. Now, what do you think of that, eh?"

"I think," Chessie said, "that you're coming for dinner tomorrow night!"

"It's a date," said Gauss. Just before he drove off, he stuck his head out the window and said, "By the way—tell your friend Diggy that I'll be seeing him soon, okay?"

"What for?" cried Chessie, but the car had already pulled away.

9

☐ "So Phillips confessed," the judge said. "His conscience, no doubt. Guilt is like a terrible stomachache. You'd do anything to get rid of it." With a smile he leaned forward to refill Diggy's cup.

It was Saturday morning, and they were sitting in the study drinking hot chocolate. The judge leaned back in his armchair and gazed out the window. He seemed in no hurry to get to the reason for his invitation.

"I'm glad," he said, "that you didn't break into the computer. I was worried about that. It would have ruined any chance of convicting Baring. With Phillips's confession, everything will work out fine."

Diggy twisted uncomfortably in his chair. It had been a very near thing. Suppose Phillips had not been frightened enough to confess? What would the gang have done then? Oh, well, he decided, the judge was right. It had all worked out for the best.

But why had the judge called him here today? He had phoned Diggy earlier that morning and asked him to drop by. So far they had just sipped hot chocolate and chatted.

The doorbell rang, and Mrs. Emily, the housekeeper, could be heard in the hallway. There was a murmur of voices, the sound of footsteps, and Diggy turned as Sergeant Gauss walked into the room.

"Come in, Sergeant," Judge Jarrell said, rising. "I think you've met young Caldwell." Gauss grunted a greeting and sat down in an armchair facing them. The judge offered him some hot chocolate, but the sergeant grimaced and shook his head. He took a notebook from his pocket and opened it.

"You're interested in this Baring case, Judge," he said, "so here's the latest. When this guy, Phillips, walked in and started babbling about how his boss was swindling people, it was a real shocker. We don't usually have cases like this solved for us so neatly. The D.A. issued a warrant for Baring's arrest and sent three men down to pick the guy up at his office. When they got there, the secretary said that Baring was having lunch at his club. When the three detectives got to the club, however, not only was Baring not there, but he wasn't even expected. No reservation for lunch. By the time our men got to his apartment, the place was empty."

The judge frowned. "So Baring has disappeared."

"Flown the coop. And the secretary, too. Both on their way to Brazil right now, I bet."

"Why Brazil?" Diggy asked.

"There's no way he can be brought back from there," the judge explained. "We have no treaty with Brazil that requires them to return fugitives from justice."

"But the Xuans' money! Can't that be recovered?"

Sergeant Gauss grinned. "The judge didn't tell you? We have the money. Phillips gave us the name of the bank and the phony name Baring used for the account. Baring can't get a penny of that money without being arrested."

Diggy sat back in his chair. "So the Xuans will get all their savings back?"

"As soon as Baring is caught, tried, and found guilty of cheating them," Gauss said. "And now, you might be wondering why the judge and I arranged to see you here. Well, it's not just to tell you the good news about the money. It seems that Phillips hadn't been sleeping too well before he came in to confess. He kept telling my men about strange phone calls in the night. Voices telling him the jig

was up, that he'd better confess. He was hysterical
. . . sounded almost like he had had a vision. We
couldn't make any sense out of the whole thing.
Maybe you could help us, Caldwell . . . got any
idea what might have made Phillips hear voices in
the middle of the night?"

Diggy took a swallow of his hot chocolate. "You
know, Sergeant Gauss," he said, "guilt is just like a
terrible stomachache. You'd do anything to get rid
of it." The judge choked, and Sergeant Gauss
looked confused. "I guess a guilty man can imagine
all sorts of weird things," Diggy added.

The sergeant shook his head, and Judge Jarrell
leaned forward with a chuckle to refill the boy's
cup.

"Okay, Diggy," said Gauss, "you know neither
the judge nor I can prove anything. But my opinion
is that you kids cut it awfully fine. You're their
leader, Caldwell, the one they look up to. Sure, you
were on the right side this time, trying to help the
Xuans—but I'm just telling you to be careful.
We're going to forget about that black box and
those telephone calls that Phillips was talking
about. Okay? But just take it easy . . . understood?"

Ten minutes later Diggy and Sergeant Gauss left
the house and walked down the street. The sergeant was in a relaxed mood, and as they strolled
along he told Diggy what it had been like growing
up there forty years ago.

"This is my town," the sergeant said. "I was born right here in Society Hill. Sounds real ritzy, doesn't it? Well, I'll tell you, it wasn't. You probably know how it got its name, from a bunch of colonial merchants called the Society of Traders. But in my day it was a tough neighborhood—Irish, Polish, Italian, Jewish, and blacks. Any kid who got into trouble was taken behind the woodshed by his father and taught just how to behave. My old man and I made that trip more than once."

They crossed the street and the sergeant stopped to light a cigar. "This was no resort then. Old buildings, empty lots filled with junk, run-down warehouses. When I got back from Vietnam, they had torn down the old neighborhood and put up all this fake colonial stuff."

They were walking past a construction site bordered by a high wooden wall. Today was Saturday, and the bulldozers were silent. Another piece of the sergeant's old neighborhood is disappearing, Diggy thought. He peered through a small opening cut into the wall. He could see a large gaping hole in the earth, a few steel girders, and some big equipment. The usual scene . . . but as Diggy looked he realized there was something on the far side of the site that was not usual. Two figures were struggling violently next to the truck entrance.

Diggy cried out, "Sergeant, it's *Chessie!*"

Gauss pushed him aside and stared through the

hole. Then with a curse he threw away his cigar and began to run along the wall. For a stocky man, he was fast, and Diggy had to race to keep up. They pelted around the corner and saw the truck gate about a block away.

"Chessie! We're coming!" Diggy yelled. They were fifty yards from the entrance when a black-coated figure with long dark hair came running out of the site and vanished around the corner.

"Chessie! Chessie!" Gasping for breath, they reached the gate and swung through it.

The girl was sprawled on the muddy ground just inside the gate. She was sobbing, tears mixing with the dirt on her face. She tried to talk, but only choking sounds came out.

Sergeant Gauss helped her to her feet and put his arms around her. "Okay, Francesca, it's all right. It's all over now."

Chessie took several deep breaths. She touched her face and said, sniffling, "Gee, I must be a mess."

"Tell me what happened." The sergeant produced a large handkerchief and began to wipe her face.

"It was Selma!" Chessie wailed.

"Baring's secretary?"

"That's right. She must have followed me from my house. The first thing I knew, she grabbed me from behind and pushed me into this place."

"How'd she know where you live?"

"It's my own fault. I forgot that my name and address is on the order form inside the cookie boxes I sold her. How stupid can you get? She had my arm twisted behind me and was screaming in my ear. I tried to get away but she kept squeezing my arm until it hurt. It must be all black and blue. Some Girl Scout *she* must have been!"

Chessie blew her nose into the handkerchief and looked angrily at the rip in her jeans. "My mother will kill me for this."

"I'll explain to your family," said the sergeant. "What did that woman want?"

"She wanted to know where Phillips was hiding. Can you imagine? She thought *I* knew where he is. I kept telling her I didn't know, but she didn't believe me. She said Baring wouldn't hurt him. She told me to find out from my friends in the police station and get the message to Phillips to deny everything. Baring would give him a lot of money. She said if I didn't, she'd come back and really hurt me."

Sergeant Gauss glanced around. "Diggy, take Chessie home and tell her mother I'll be there later. I've got to get to a telephone."

Diggy nodded, taking Chessie's arm. "So it's not Brazil, huh, sergeant? That crook and his secretary are still in town."

"Let's go," said Gauss. "I'll walk you to the corner."

□

Frankie Morelli was inspecting the neighborhood through his new telescope when Chessie and Diggy approached the house. He whistled softly as he took in his sister's dirty face and torn jeans. Chessie was limping from a stone in her shoe and she paused to get rid of it.

Frankie grinned. Running up to Diggy, he took his telescope and hit him in the stomach. "That'll teach you not to pick on girls!" he yelled. Diggy doubled over and stepped back a few paces.

"*Frankie!*" Chessie screamed. "Diggy didn't have anything to do with it! Now come back and apologize, or I'll tell Mom!"

"When Mom gets home," Frankie sneered, "you won't have a chance to squeal. You're gonna catch it good."

"Diggy, are you all right?" asked Chessie.

"Yeah, but I'm going to teach that little monster a lesson." Diggy ran forward, and scooping Frankie up in his arms, held him upside down until he shrieked for mercy.

"Had enough, tough guy?"

Chessie laughed. "I don't know which of you is worse. Frankie, c'mon inside with me. And I don't want Mom hearing about how I look, okay?"

Diggy set the little boy down, and with an impish grin Frankie bounced into the house. He had already decided what his sister would have to give him to keep him quiet.

□

"I got cleaned up and hid my clothes away just before my mother got home," Chessie said. "I had to give that little brat one of my *Star Trek* posters to get him to shut up, but it was worth it."

It was Sunday afternoon, and they had met in the clubhouse to celebrate. Chessie had been the last to arrive, but she was bursting with news.

"When Sergeant Gauss showed up a little while later and told my parents what had happened, I thought my father was going to explode. I really did. My mother just looked grim—her I'll-speak-to-you-later-young-lady look. Anyway, the sergeant was really nice about it. He laid it on thick, how brave I was, how we had solved this case and helped the Xuans. Luckily he didn't say how we did it."

"You think he knows?" Bobbie asked.

"I'm sure of it," Diggy said. "The judge knows too."

"But the big news came later," said Chessie. She paused, and all the kids leaned forward.

"The police arrested Baring this morning!"

Cheers and shouts filled the garage.

"How did they get him?" asked Larry.

"Well, when the sergeant left me and Diggy yesterday, he called the police station. Ten minutes later a squad car on patrol spotted Selma getting into a rented car two blocks from my house. They grabbed her before she could get away." Chessie laughed. "But the best thing was how cool she was about it. She wouldn't say a word to anybody, just kept asking for her lawyer. Claimed she didn't know where Baring was, and that she had never been near me. Sergeant Gauss said they couldn't get a word out of her."

Sphinx grinned. "She didn't say she was twisting your arm in order to get more of those delicious cookies out of you?"

Chessie sighed. "I'll never feel quite the same about the Girl Scouts again."

"But what about Baring?" Tilo asked. "How did they get him?"

"Well, Selma wouldn't say anything, but they searched her purse and found a key to a motel room in the suburbs. The police watched the place all night—and early this morning, who should show up but a big man with dark black hair and horn-rimmed glasses! Guess who?"

"Baring!" five voices shouted, and Chessie nodded, laughing. "The very same. His disguise didn't help him. Right now he and his nasty girlfriend are behind bars."

There were more cheers. "I wonder why he didn't run when he had the chance?" Bobbie asked.

"Oh, guys like Baring always think they're smarter than anyone else," Larry said. "Besides, where could he go with no money?"

Diggy nodded. "He thought he could scare Phillips into denying everything he had said. Then the police wouldn't have a shred of proof."

"Well," sighed Bobbie, "it all worked out, anyway."

Tilo had one last surprise for them.

"My parents and I would like to thank you for all you've done," he said shyly. "Please come to our house for a tea party next Sunday at four. My parents want to thank you personally. We are very grateful."

It was almost five o'clock when they finally left the garage. They walked through Independence Hall Park, stopping to admire the historic building with its arrow-shaped white steeple and old-fashioned clock. There were the small round windows from which the Founding Fathers had looked out on Philadelphia. And there was the statue of Admiral Barry—no, Diggy insisted, Commodore Barry—on the lawn, pointing south towards an invisible enemy.

"Well, we've provided for the common defense, too," Bobbie said.

"And assured domestic tranquillity in the Xuan family," Larry added.

"And we made sure," Diggy said, "that at least one crook will be deprived of his liberty!"

Tilo stood, gazing across the lawn. "Is there not something also about forming a more perfect union?"

"Oh," said Sphinx with a grin, "that's the Galaxy Gang. That's us!"